Silver medal winner of
the Key Colors Competition USA, 2020

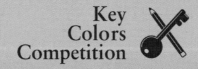

Soomi's Sweater written and illustrated by Susie Oh

ISBN 978-1-60537-691-2

This book was printed in June 2021 at Nikara, M. R. Štefánika 858/25, 963 01 Krupina, Slovakia.

First Edition
10 9 8 7 6 5 4 3 2 1

SOOMI'S SWEATER

Susie Oh

Clavis

NEW YORK

Soomi's new sweater arrives
in a box with soft, crinkly paper.

It's blue-green

with two yellow stripes,

three yellow buttons,

and a small pocket.

It's too big to wear now,
but Mom says it'll fit when Soomi

IS
THIS TALL.

But Soomi can't wait!
She begs and pleads until

Mom rolls up the too-long sleeves.

She pins up the too-long hem.
Now it's a near perfect fit.

Soomi is excited to show off
her new sweater at school.

When she rushes to throw off her jacket, it snags on her sleeve.

A little thread unravels and . . .

. . . tangles and . . .

. . . tears loose.

Soomi has ripped
HER NEW SWEATER.

She stares at the raggedy hole
and wonders what to do.

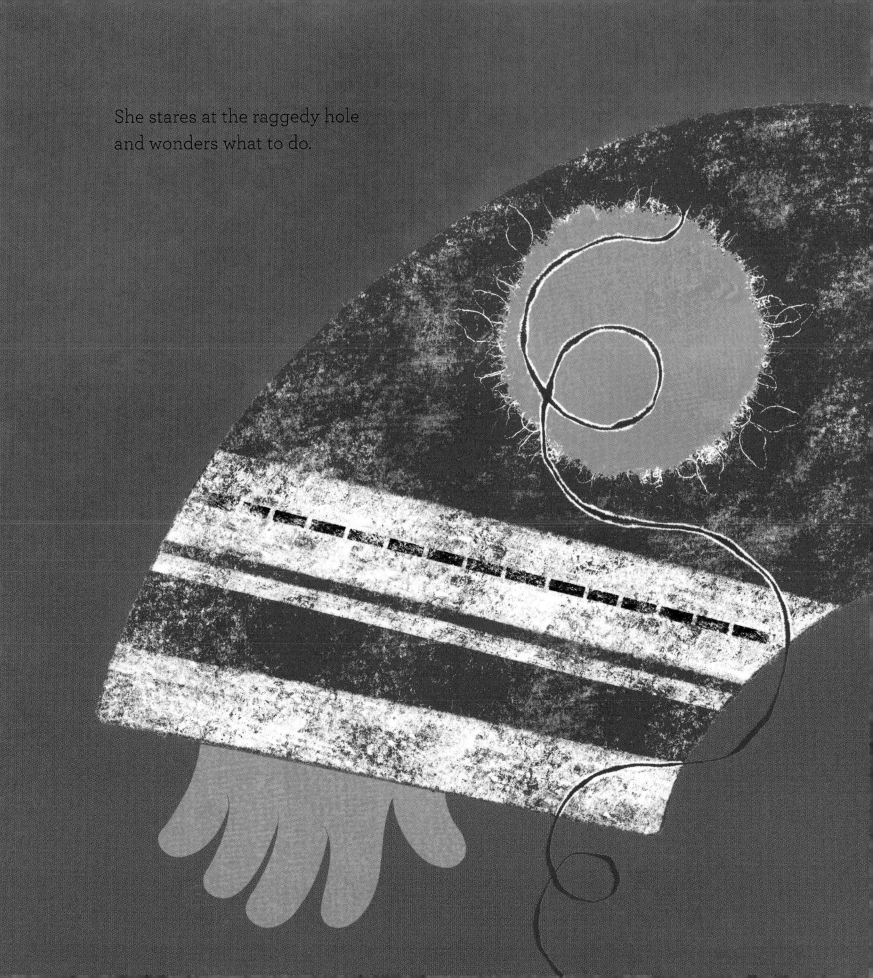

Soomi's friends see she's upset,
and they want to help.

Will a **BAND-AID** fix the rip?

Can **STICKY TAPE** repair the tear?

Will **GLUE** seal the split?

Now Soomi doesn't have just
a hole in her sleeve. She has a

STICKY,
GOOEY,
RAGGED,
GLOOPY,
MESSY,
TATTERED

hole in her sleeve.

She's had
ENOUGH.

Soomi is afraid
to show Mom
her torn sweater.

But Mom says,
"This big rip is only
a small problem to mend."

Mom finds a sewing kit and an old shirt that Soomi outgrew.

First, Mom cuts out a patch of fabric.

Next, she places the patch under the hole.

Then, she threads a needle.

She stitches in
 and out
  and over
    and under.

At last, she sews
a butterfly onto the patch,
and the sweater is
BETTER THAN NEW.

Soomi loves her better-than-new sweater.
She'll save it to wear when

SHE'S
THIS TALL.